To: M

Barbie™
Mariposa
& the
Fairy Princess

The Junior Novelization

From:
Ms. Hoffman

June 2024

Special thanks to Diane Reichenberger, Cindy Ledermann, Jocelyn Morgan,
Kim Culmone, Tanya Mann, Emily Kelly, Sharon Woloszyk, Carla Alford,
Rita Lichtwardt, Kathy Berry, Rob Hudnut, David Wiebe, Shelley Dvi-Vardhana,
Gabrielle Miles, Rainmaker Entertainment, and Walter P. Martishius

Published in the United States by Random House Children's Books, a division of
Random House, Inc., 1745 Broadway, New York, NY 10019, and in Canada by
Random House of Canada Limited, Toronto. Random House and the colophon
are registered trademarks of Random House, Inc.
ISBN 978-0-449-81635-6
randomhouse.com/kids
Printed in the United States of America
10 9 8 7 6 5 4 3 2 1   First Edition

The Junior Novelization

Adapted by Molly McGuire Woods
Based on the screenplay by Elise Allen
Illustrated by Ulkutay Design Group

Random House New York

Sparkle
Barbie
Let your dreams
Always be...
real fairy princess in you!
adventure lead the way! Let the
Be yourself
Shimmer, Flutter! Sparkle,
A Princess Never Hides Her Wings
If you be
A Pri
Sparkle, Shimmer, Flutter!
If you believe it, you will Soar!
Be A Friend
To M...
Love the
Sparkle!
Barbie
Th
Wings
If you believe it, you will Soar!
To Make A Friend...Be A Friend
Let y...
The secret to a great
friendship
is being a great friend!
Barbie
ams soar!
...be true to the real fairy princess
the adventure
Love the
...kle!
nd
Wings

Chapter 1

Mariposa the Butterfly Fairy flapped her delicate shimmering wings and soared through the sky. She tilted her head toward the sun to feel its warmth on her cheeks and took a deep breath, smelling the sweet scent of flowers wafting up from the fields below. Mariposa grinned at her best friend, Willa, who was gliding along beside her. What a lovely morning in Flutterfield!

The two Butterfly Fairies were headed to the palace, where Mariposa worked in the royal library. The morning flight with Willa was Mariposa's favorite part of the day. It gave the friends a chance to catch up and take in the beauty of their city.

The girls weren't the only fairies out and about on such a glorious morning. The sky buzzed with activity as fairies zipped this way and that, carrying backpacks, briefcases, and breakfast. While the passersby might have been headed to different places, they all seemed to recognize Mariposa.

"Morning, Mariposa!" one fairy called.

"Hi, Mariposa! Thanks for the suggestion on the book!" another shouted across the sky.

Mariposa nodded and waved to each passing fairy. She had to admit, she was something of a celebrity in Flutterfield these days. It was all because of the Skeezites, scary monsters who preyed on Butterfly Fairies. Recently, the Skeezites had threatened to attack Flutterfield. But with the help of her fairy friends, Mariposa had returned the city to safety. Ever since then, she had been getting a lot of attention. It seemed she couldn't go anywhere without someone recognizing her.

"Excuse me, Mariposa?" a woman called from behind them.

Mariposa and Willa turned and saw the woman hovering nearby with a young girl.

"Yes?" Mariposa replied, stopping to talk.

"Sorry to bother you," the fairy began, "but I was hoping you might have a chance to say hello. My daughter is a big fan."

"Of me?" Mariposa asked, flattered.

The little fairy girl nodded vigorously. "I know all about how you and your friends got the big, scary Skeezites out of Flutterfield," she announced.

Mariposa gave the girl a warm smile. "Oh, it wasn't just me. There were lots of fairies who helped. Willa helped," she explained, pointing to her best friend.

The little fairy girl leaned close to Mariposa. "Is it true you've read every book in Flutterfield?" she asked in an awed whisper.

Mariposa let out a laugh. She did love to read, but she wasn't sure *anyone* could read all the books in their enormous royal library! "Well, not every one," she answered with a wink. "But there's still time."

The fairy girl giggled and then rooted around in her schoolbag. She pulled out a quill and a notebook. "Will you sign my book?" she asked eagerly.

"Really? Okay," Mariposa said, feeling slightly embarrassed. This wasn't the first time someone had asked for her autograph, but it still felt strange that so many people should know her. She wasn't sure she'd ever get used to it. Nevertheless, she took the quill, turned to a fresh notebook page, and began to sign her name.

"And whenever you're looking for book recommendations," she added, handing the notebook back to the girl, "come by the royal library in the palace. I'm there every day."

The fairy girl excitedly clutched her notebook to her chest. "I will, for sure! Thanks so much, Mariposa!" she exclaimed. "Bye!"

The mother fairy reached for Mariposa's hand. "Thank you," she said gratefully.

Mariposa waved to them both as they flew away. It sure was fun getting to stop and speak with so many of the citizens of Flutterfield. Being famous had its perks!

Just then, Willa's voice snapped Mariposa back to reality. "Hey! How come I never get an autograph?" she whined, pretending to pout.

Mariposa grinned and poked her best friend playfully in the arm. "Because you never have a pen!" she joked.

The two friends cracked up and continued flying to the palace.

"You must be the most famous librarian ever," Willa said.

"Royal *historian*," Mariposa corrected her. "And I chose the best job in the world. I get to spend all day with the biggest book collection in Flutterfield—it's perfect!"

The girls flapped their shimmering wings and flew high above a field of gorgeous Flutter Flowers. Suddenly, they heard a loud screech.

EEEEEEEEEEEEEEEKKK!

Mariposa stopped and looked around. She spotted a familiar furry pink puffball racing through the sky. It darted this way and that, almost knocking over several fairies as it barreled right toward Mariposa. She braced herself as the high-energy puffball crashed right into her knees.

"Easy, Zee!" she said, laughing and helping her bubbly pet puffball steady herself.

Zee flapped her arms and squeaked loudly. Mariposa! she seemed to say.

"I'm right here. What is it?"

Zee jumped up and down wildly and pointed toward the castle.

Mariposa furrowed her brow and focused. What was Zee trying to tell her? "The queen wants to see me right away?"

Zee nodded.

"Did she say why?" Mariposa asked.

Zee shrugged. She didn't know. Maybe the queen was planning on throwing Mariposa a surprise party. She pretended to hide and then yell *Surprise!*

"That *would* be a surprise," said Willa, "since it's not Mariposa's birthday."

Mariposa giggled. There was only one thing to do. "Let's go find out!" she cried. "Zee, lead the way!"

Chapter 2

At the palace a short while later, Mariposa carefully opened the door to the throne room and stepped inside. Willa and Zee followed.

Zee gave a low whistle. *Check this place out!*

Mariposa looked around the lavishly decorated space and let out a breath. Even though she came to the palace every day for work, she rarely had a chance to leave the library. She couldn't believe that such a beautiful room had been right around the corner all this time!

She tried to calm her nerves by taking a deep breath. Mariposa knew that Queen Marabella ruled her kingdom with kindness, but still, it wasn't every day that the queen summoned her.

At the far end of the long, narrow room,

Mariposa saw two large, regal thrones. Queen Marabella sat in one. Her son, Prince Carlos, sat in the other, and Lord Gastrous stood nearby. The queen motioned Mariposa forward.

"Mariposa," she said in a warm voice. "Thank you for coming."

"Of course, Your Majesty," Mariposa replied, curtsying deeply. She turned to the prince and repeated her curtsy. "Prince Carlos."

"Good morning, Mariposa," the prince replied smoothly.

Lord Gastrous cleared his throat arrogantly. "Ahem," he said, glaring at Mariposa.

"Oh!" Mariposa exclaimed. She was so nervous, she'd almost forgotten to curtsy in his direction as well. "Lord Gastrous," she said, sinking down extra low to make it up to him.

The lord gave her a smug nod.

Queen Marabella spoke. "Mariposa, tell me, what do you know about Crystal Fairies?"

Mariposa bit her lip. "The Crystal Fairies? From Shimmervale?"

Zee wrinkled her nose and stuck out her

tongue. *Crystal Fairies—yuck!*

Mariposa thought for a moment. She wasn't sure why the queen would be asking her about Crystal Fairies, although from her reading, she had learned a fair amount about them. She wondered which facts the queen would be most interested in.

"Well," she began, "their land is built on an amazing natural energy source called Crystallites, and the Crystallites heat and power everything in their realm."

Carlos leaned toward the queen. "I told you she'd be the perfect choice," he whispered.

"Hardly," Lord Gastrous grumped. "She hasn't mentioned that they're vicious, vile, and the sworn enemies of the Butterfly Fairies."

Mariposa cleared her throat timidly. "With all due respect, Lord Gastrous, I don't believe that to be true." All of her reading had shown her that the Crystal Fairies were peaceful. But she knew many citizens of Flutterfield distrusted them.

"Aha! You see?" Lord Gastrous said, waving

an annoyed finger in the air. "Misinformation! I've been around long enough to know who our enemies are."

Willa tugged on her best friend's arm. "Mariposa, Crystal Fairies are scary and cruel," she said.

"Only because that's what we've been led to believe," Mariposa replied. "It's what's in our fairy tales. But the real history is different. Look."

Mariposa walked toward a thick, ancient-looking book resting on a table nearby. She opened the book to a picture of Crystal Fairies and Butterfly Fairies dancing together in front of a beautiful shimmering waterfall.

"Centuries ago," she continued, showing the picture to the queen, "Butterfly Fairies and Crystal Fairies were allies. Then the Crystal Fairies accused the Butterfly Fairies of trying to steal their Crystallites." She turned the page. "The Butterfly Fairies denied it, the Crystal Fairies didn't believe them, and everyone got angrier and angrier. Then the two sides declared themselves eternal enemies and vowed never to have contact again."

Willa took the book from Mariposa and leafed through it. "Okay," she said. "But what about the part where the Crystal Fairies grind Butterfly Fairy wings to make their bread? Where's the picture of that?"

Mariposa shook her head. "You won't find it; never happened," she said matter-of-factly.

Lord Gastrous pounded his fist on the arm of his throne. "Preposterous! Your Majesty, the girl has no idea what she's talking about!"

"But I *do*!" Mariposa exclaimed, taking a step forward. "Your Majesty, all the horrible stories about Crystal Fairies are just that: *stories*."

Queen Marabella nodded approvingly. "And that's exactly the thing on which we should base our decisions: research, not hearsay." She cast a sideways glance at Lord Gastrous. "I'm convinced," she announced, fixing her gaze on Mariposa. "You shall leave for Shimmervale as Flutterfield's royal ambassador at once. You will live with their royal family for one week and prove that Butterfly Fairies and Crystal Fairies can be friends."

Mariposa's mouth dropped open. *Her? A royal ambassador?*

Zee pretended to faint.

"But Crystal Fairies are dangerous!" Willa protested. "If Mariposa goes there, she'll be—"

"Welcomed as an honored guest," Queen Marabella interrupted. "That's what King Regellius assured me."

"The Crystal Fairies will love you, Mariposa. I know it," Prince Carlos added, trying to reassure her.

Mariposa could feel everyone's eyes on her. She knew they were expecting her to go along with the plan. After all, it was a royal request. But Mariposa was unsure. What if she let the queen—and the city of Flutterfield—down?

"But who will look after the royal library?" she asked, stalling.

"Willa can manage it," the queen replied.

"She can?" Mariposa asked uncertainly.

"I can?" Willa echoed.

"Of course she can," Prince Carlos declared. "And I will help also."

Mariposa wrung her hands. She was honored that the queen thought she could perform such an important job. But it all was happening so fast! She'd never traveled alone outside of Flutterfield before. What if she got lost? What if they didn't like her? She took a deep breath.

"I—" she started. "I'm sorry. I can't." She covered her face with her hands and raced from the throne room.

Chapter 3

A little while later, Mariposa sat in her favorite thinking spot on the outskirts of Flutterfield with Zee curled up in her lap. Mariposa loved to watch the stars from there. Their twinkling always seemed to calm her.

Suddenly, a familiar voice broke through the quiet. "Ah, Willa told me I'd find you here."

Mariposa turned toward her visitor. "Hello, Carlos," she said.

The prince sat on the soft ivy leaves next to Mariposa and was quiet for a moment. Then he asked, "Why won't you go to Shimmervale?"

Mariposa stopped petting Zee and sighed. Carlos had asked the question she'd been dreading all afternoon. "I don't think I'm ambassador material," she admitted softly.

Prince Carlos looked surprised. "But you're the smartest fairy I know!" he cried. "You've read every book on Shimmervale."

"Yeah, I'm great with books," Mariposa replied. "But making peace with the Crystal Fairies? I can't do that."

"I know you'll win them over," Carlos insisted.

Mariposa shook her head, unconvinced. "But what if I don't? What if I say or do the wrong thing? What if I make things worse?"

It was Carlos's turn to shake his head. "You won't," he said confidently. "We all believe in you. Just be yourself. And remember, the best way to make a friend is to be a friend."

Mariposa thought about that. It was good advice. Still, she wasn't sure she had enough courage.

"Oh," Carlos continued. "I almost forgot. My mother asked me to give you this." He reached into his satchel and pulled out a delicate, glowing flower.

Mariposa gently took the flower in her hands, feeling the warmth of its light.

"It's beautiful," she whispered.

Zee's eyes bulged out of her head. *Wow! Beautiful is right!*

"It's a Flutter Flower," Carlos explained. "It's made from the most precious magic of Flutterfield. Whenever you have doubts, just take it out and it will remind you of us."

Mariposa smiled. Somehow, looking at the Flutter Flower's beauty made her realize just how important this mission was. She had a chance to help others appreciate what made Flutterfield special. How could she pass that up?

Mariposa straightened her shoulders and looked Carlos in the eyes. "Okay," she said, determined. "I'll go to Shimmervale."

Carlos pumped his fist in the air: Yes! He took her hand in his and laid out the plan. "You'll be welcomed on the outskirts of town," he explained.

Mariposa nodded. Her mind was already racing with everything she needed to do to get ready.

"Guess I'll see you when I get back, then,"

she said, gliding into the air with Zee at her side. "Bye, Carlos."

"Good-bye!" Carlos called. "And good luck!"

I'll need it, Mariposa thought.

Back in her room with Willa and Zee, Mariposa stared at her bookshelf. She tried to decide which books to pack for her trip to Shimmervale. But it was impossible to narrow down the list, so she just grabbed as many as she could carry. Then she turned to Willa and continued her instructions.

"Okay. Monday, the new manuscripts come in. On Tuesdays and Thursdays, you need to lead guided tours. On Wednesdays, the tapestries get touched up and cleaned, and on Friday, we read books to the elderly," she said.

Mariposa hoped Willa was paying attention. Leaving the library in someone else's hands— even if they were her best friend's—was stressing her out! "Willa, did you get all that?"

Willa looked up from the notebook she was

furiously scribbling in. "Yes. I think so," she said unsurely. "What was that thing you said? After 'Monday'?"

Smiling, Mariposa rolled her eyes and blew out a breath. She would just have to trust that the library would still be standing when she returned. She flew to her suitcase with her pile of books and dumped them in. "There!" she exclaimed, brushing her hands together. "Is there anything I forgot?"

Willa and Zee looked at her suitcase overflowing with nothing but books.

"Um . . . ," Willa started, "your clothes?"

Mariposa slapped her forehead. "Oh. Right," she said sheepishly. "Hmm." She eyed her suitcase. There didn't seem to be any room!

"I'm on it," Willa announced, taking charge. She zoomed around the room and returned to the suitcase with a little pile of clothes. She moved aside a few books and stuffed the clothes in a small corner. Now all they had to do was close it. First Willa tried sitting on the suitcase. Then she tried jumping on it. But it was no use—the suitcase was too full!

She motioned for Mariposa and Zee to help. Working together, they shoved and squeezed until finally they managed to close the suitcase.

Willa wiped her forehead. "Piece of cake!" she said, trying to catch her breath.

Mariposa giggled. "Thanks," she said, hugging Willa. "Wish me luck!"

"Good luck. Be careful, okay?" Willa replied.

"I will!"

Mariposa gave her friend one last hug and turned to leave. "Okay, Zee," she called over her shoulder. "We're ready to go. Zee?" Mariposa looked around for her favorite pink puffball but didn't see her anywhere.

Willa motioned toward the bookshelf.

Mariposa spied one loose book suspiciously moving all by itself toward the door. "Zee?" she called in the book's direction, winking at Willa.

The book froze for a second, and then Zee peeked over the edge.

"Zee, are you hiding?" Mariposa asked.

Zee shrugged and blushed. *Maybe?*

Mariposa crouched down. "You're not afraid of the Crystal Fairies, are you?" she asked.

Zee shook her head back and forth. *No.* Then she shook it up and down. *Yes.* She didn't know! *Maybe?*

Mariposa patted her head reassuringly. "Zee, it'll be fine. There are no stories about Crystal Fairies eating puffballs. C'mon! Let's have an adventure!"

Zee nodded in agreement.

Satisfied, Mariposa spun into the air. "Bye, Willa!" She flew toward the door and then looked over her shoulder.

Zee hid behind Willa and waved as if she wasn't going anywhere. That silly puffball!

"Come on," Mariposa said, pulling Zee out from behind Willa.

A moment later, they set out on their adventure.

Chapter 4

Mariposa and Zee soared high above the hills of Flutterfield, marveling at the beauty of their home. *I sure will miss the flowers while I'm gone,* Mariposa thought. She wondered if Shimmervale had flowers of its own.

Zee darted in front of Mariposa and giggled. The puffball tapped her playfully on the wing. *Tag! You're it!*

Mariposa laughed and raced to catch Zee.

That evening, Mariposa and Zee stopped to rest in a part of Fairytopia called Atlantis. They'd made a tent using a canopy of leaves and flowers and were nestled cozily inside.

As Zee snored softly next to her, Mariposa opened a book and began to study. "*Shimmervale: A History* says 'Diplomats to Shimmervale receive a grand welcome, including a parade, marching band, and fireworks,'" she read aloud.

Well, that sounds nice, Mariposa thought.

The next day, Mariposa took out her map to check their location. By her calculations, they should have been near the Shimmervale meeting spot Carlos had described. She shielded her eyes against the sun's glare and scanned their surroundings. Sure enough, she spotted the landmark she had been looking for and headed toward it.

"This is the meeting spot, Zee!" Mariposa cried excitedly. But something wasn't right. The place was deserted. Where could everybody be? Mariposa checked the sun. "We're right on time," she reasoned.

Zee raised an eyebrow. *Some welcome committee! What about the parade and the band?*

Suddenly, *SNAP!*—a twig broke nearby, cracking loudly against the quiet.

Zee jumped into Mariposa's arms with fear.

"Is someone there? Hello?" Mariposa asked timidly. She didn't see anyone, but she thought she heard a rustling in the bushes. She set Zee on the ground and walked slowly and cautiously toward the sound. Zee bit her nails and hid behind Mariposa's legs. With one finger, Mariposa carefully pulled back a branch.

"Don't hurt me!" cried a frightened voice.

"Of course we won't hurt you," Mariposa replied, relieved to find a small fairy, about her age, hiding there. "I'm Mariposa, from Flutterfield, and this is Zee." She pointed to her puffball, who was now bravely poking out her chest.

"You're not going to hypnotize me with your wicked magic, then lure me back to your dark, dismal cave?"

"Um . . . no?" Mariposa replied, confused.

The fairy looked relieved and stood up, shaking out her wings. "Oh, goody. I'm Talayla," she said, offering her hand to shake. Then she gasped. "Your butterfly wings are so beautiful!"

"Thank you," Mariposa said, noticing Talayla's

smaller, shimmering wings. "I like yours, too."

Talayla crouched down next to Zee. "Look! How cute!" She reached out to pet her. "Is that your war beast?" she asked, pulling back, evidently thinking twice.

Zee looked down at her round tummy and fluffy fur. *Do I look like a war beast?*

"No," Mariposa answered.

It sure seemed like Talayla had a lot of misinformation about Butterfly Fairies. It made Mariposa think of Lord Gastrous back home.

"Then, yay!" Talayla squealed, tickling Zee behind the ears. "How cute!"

Mariposa looked at their abandoned surroundings. "So . . . is this the grand welcome?" she asked hesitantly.

Talayla dug her foot into the dirt and looked embarrassed. "Oh, that. The flying band was too afraid to come meet you."

"Ah," Mariposa said. It looked like the fairies of Flutterfield weren't the only ones who could make up stories. She tried not to take it personally. "It's okay."

"Come on," Talayla said. "I'll show you both all around Shimmervale! I mean"—she cleared her throat and continued, in a very official-sounding voice—"in the name of his Royal King Regellius, it is my privilege to give you an official tour of our fairy land." Then she giggled with excitement and shot into the air. "Let's go!"

Mariposa and Zee exchanged a look. So far, their welcoming committee wasn't what they had expected! They wondered what other surprises Shimmervale had in store.

Chapter 5

Talayla zoomed across the sky, pointing out landmarks left and right. She flew so fast Mariposa and Zee struggled to keep up!

"Welcome to Shimmervale," Talayla called over her shoulder.

Mariposa tried to take in her surroundings as she flew. Shimmervale was a bustling city with lots of fairies fluttering about. There were many homes, all with rocks glowing warmly on their roofs. *Those must be the Crystallites*, thought Mariposa.

"I see every roof has a Crystallite," Mariposa stated matter-of-factly, eager to show off her knowledge of Shimmervale. "The main source of heat and power here in Shimmer—"

Talayla stopped in her tracks and shot

Mariposa a look. "Uh, that's *my* line?"

"Sorry."

"As you can see," Talayla continued, "every roof has a Crystallite, the main source of heat and power here in Shimmervale." And with that, she darted off to the next location.

Mariposa glanced at Zee and shrugged. They'd better keep up if they didn't want to be left behind!

The next stop on the tour was a grassy area dotted with purple plants. It looked just like one of the places Mariposa had read about in her books.

"Featherfrond Fields!" Talayla announced, sweeping her arm through the air.

Zee flew to Mariposa's side, panting and trying to catch her breath. This tour was wearing her out!

Mariposa nodded. "I understand some of the Crystal Fairies use the purple featherfronds to make dye for their clothi—"

"Next stop, Glow Water Falls and the palace!" Talayla interrupted, zipping away again.

Mariposa felt flustered. She only wanted to show Talayla that she had done her homework. But it didn't look like their tour guide was interested. *Oh well,* she thought as she once again rose into the air.

Zee let out an exhausted sigh and followed. Being a tourist was hard work!

After some time, the fairies and Zee rounded a corner. Talayla stopped short.

"Here it is: Glow Water Falls!" she announced triumphantly.

Not paying attention, Mariposa flew along, reading one of her Shimmervale guidebooks. "Historians say—"

"Historians say this is where Shimmervale's first residents discovered Crystallites," Talayla finished. She wasn't going to let Mariposa be the guide on this tour!

Mariposa shut her book in frustration. But she forgot all about it when she looked up. "Whoa!" she breathed.

Glow Water Falls was stunning! Everywhere Mariposa looked, water flowed over glowing

Crystallites. The palace itself stood off in the distance. "I never thought I'd say this, but pictures don't do it justice," Mariposa admitted.

"Yup," Talayla agreed, taking in the scenery and looking as awed as Mariposa. "That's why we end the tour here."

Zee flew up next to Mariposa, gasping for breath.

"Zee? Are you okay?" Mariposa asked, reaching out to pet the puffball.

Zee tried to respond but held up one finger instead. *Hang on a minute. Let me just catch my breath.* She mopped the sweat from her brow with Mariposa's skirt.

"Awwww," Talayla cooed. "Am I going too fast for you, little puffer?"

Zee nodded and then collapsed dramatically into Mariposa's arms.

Mariposa smiled and rolled her eyes. "No, she's fine," she said to Talayla.

Zee lifted her head and gave Mariposa a sideways glance. *Can't you see I'm dying here?* She groaned and fell backward again.

Talayla clapped her hands. "And now on to the palace, where you'll be staying." With that, she zipped off, leaving them behind.

Mariposa and Zee exchanged a look, then hurried after Talayla. As they neared the castle, they heard a voice overhead.

"Hey," the voice whispered.

Mariposa looked around. Was the voice talking to her?

"Hey!" the voice said again, louder this time.

Mariposa looked up. A few stories above, she saw a fairy about her age. She had shimmering wings and wore flowing silky robes. She waved to Mariposa.

Mariposa pointed to herself. *Me?*

The fairy nodded, and Mariposa flew up to the window, Zee trailing behind her.

"Hi," the fairy said in a friendly voice.

Just then, a furry blue-green puffball lunged out the window. It hovered in the air between the two girls, growling.

Mariposa jumped.

Zee squealed with fright.

"Anu!" the fairy scolded, pushing the puffball to the side. "You're scaring them!" Then she looked around suspiciously, as if checking to make sure they were alone. Satisfied, she continued. "You're Mariposa, aren't you? The Butterfly Fairy?" she asked in a hushed voice.

"Yes," Mariposa replied cautiously. She wasn't sure how this girl knew her, but she seemed nice enough.

"I'm Catania," the fairy announced. "It must be so terrifying, flying across Fairytopia to get here. Were you scared?"

"Scared? I don't know, it was more—"

"Catania!" a voice thundered from inside the castle. "Away from the window!"

Catania looked nervously over her shoulder. "I've got to go. Nice to meet you. Welcome to the kingdom." And with that, she vanished inside.

Anu followed Catania through the window— but not before pelting Zee in the head with a piece of fruit. *Splat!*

Zee frowned and wiped her head. *Hey!*

Mariposa watched Catania disappear and bit her lip in thought. It felt nice to finally be welcomed by someone in Shimmervale. But she couldn't shake the feeling that this place was turning out to be stranger than she'd expected.

"There you are!" cried Talayla, returning from the front of the castle to find them. "I thought I'd lost *another* visitor on the tour. I'll never live that down. Anyhoo . . . let's show you to your room."

Chapter 6

Talayla hurried Mariposa and Zee down a long hallway. Mariposa tried to take everything in and keep up at the same time. The palace was gorgeous. Everything was large, crystalline, glowing, and colorful. She hardly knew where to look first!

"...and then, you'll never guess what happened next, so good!" Talayla was babbling on. "That's when the king suggested, 'You, Talayla, would make an excellent Fairy-in-waiting.'"

Zee nodded every now and then, pretending to listen. But really, she kept ducking behind large Crystallites, marveling at how their glow changed her fur different colors.

"And now," Talayla said, pausing in front of a closed door, "ta-dah!" She flung the door open and stepped aside, sweeping her arm to showcase the room.

Mariposa and Zee peeked in and winced. The entire room was decorated like some sort of evil version of Flutterfield. All the parts were there: the Flutter Flowers, the rich colors, the trees and leaves. But it was so dark and overdone that it looked more like a haunted forest than any place that actually existed in Flutterfield.

"Wow!" Mariposa exclaimed, unsure what else to say.

Zee stuck out her tongue and turned her back on the space. *Yuck!*

"It's . . ." Mariposa struggled to find a compliment. It was obvious that someone had gone to a lot of trouble to put everything together—even if that someone thought fairies from Flutterfield were, well, evil.

"I decorated it myself!" Talayla announced proudly.

"Really? Mariposa replied, trying to find something polite to say about the crowded space. There was so much furniture it was difficult for Mariposa to move her large wings in the space. She worried she'd knock something over. She bent down to fit her wings under a tree branch sticking out from a wall.

"I based it on everything we Crystal Fairies know about Butterfly Fairies," Talayla explained.

"That was . . . thoughtful?" Mariposa replied, moving a spiky branch out of the way. *Good thing I'm here,* she thought. *Someone needs to set this story straight!*

Talayla skipped around the room, fluffing pillows and pointing out her favorite items. "Do the trees in Flutterfield really come alive, snatch fairies in midair, and devour them?" she asked.

"What?" Mariposa cried. "No!" She yanked her hand away from a tree branch. "These don't do that, do they?" she asked, giving the tree a sideways glance.

Zee moved a little closer to Mariposa just to be safe.

Talayla shook her head. "Nah," she said, sounding disappointed. "I couldn't figure out how to make it work."

Zee gave a sigh of relief and sank into a chair that resembled a bush. She immediately let out a squeak and leaped into the air.

"I *did* put in hidden thorns, though!" Talayla announced, grinning proudly.

Zee grumbled and rubbed her rear where a sharp thorn had pricked her. Some welcome party this was turning out to be!

"And now it's my extreme pleasure to invite you to meet His Royal Highness King Regellius and the Royal Princess Catania," Talayla said formally. "Unless you want to stay here and freshen up, you know, where it's familiar?"

Mariposa ducked to avoid an angry-faced tree creature looming over her. "No, uh, we will be honored to meet the king and princess." *Plus it will get us out of this room!* she added to herself.

Zee nodded in agreement. *Get me out of here!*

Talayla led Mariposa and Zee down another beautiful hallway toward the throne room. Mariposa tried to keep her palms from sweating.

Meeting the king of Shimmervale was a big deal! She wanted to make Flutterfield proud by being a good ambassador.

Talayla paused in front of another heavy door and suddenly looked nervous herself. "Now," she said, hand on the doorknob. "Please don't unleash your fire breath or anything, okay?"

"But I don't—" Mariposa began. Then she sighed. "Okay, I won't," she finished, resigned. It was going to take more time than she thought to change opinions around here.

Talayla looked relieved. "Cool," she remarked, and swung open the door. "Please welcome Mariposa, Royal Ambassador from Flutterfield," she called loudly, then announced, "Introducing King Regellius and Princess Catania!" Mariposa flew across the room toward them.

The royals were sitting side by side in some of the most beautiful, sparkling thrones Mariposa had ever seen. In fact, the entire room seemed to be gleaming, perhaps from the many Crystallites on display. Behind the princess stood a pink-and-white Pegasus. Even the horse's wings glowed from the light of the Crystallites. It neighed softly and munched on feather fronds.

As Mariposa got closer, she realized that the princess looked familiar. She was the same girl they had met at the palace window just a short while ago. Mariposa grinned, thankful for a familiar face. "Hey!" she cried, delighted.

King Regellius frowned. "Hey?" he repeated, displeased. "Is that how you address the princess of Shimmervale?"

Mariposa blushed. "No! I . . . uh . . . ," she stammered. She hadn't meant to be disrespectful. She was just excited to see Catania, who had been so kind to her earlier.

"I believe in Flutterfield 'hey' is actually a term of deep respect," Catania said, jumping to the rescue. "Isn't that right?"

Mariposa nodded enthusiastically. "Yes! Yes, it is." She threw Catania a grateful look. "Hey, Your Majesties," she continued, curtsying dramatically.

"Hey," Catania replied, nodding royally.

"Hey," the king said, still looking suspicious.

Zee zoomed up next to Mariposa and

growled at Anu, who was sitting on Catania's lap. The puffball rolled his eyes.

The king pointed a knobby finger at Zee. "Is that thing growling at me?" he asked.

"A beastly 'how are you?' in Flutterfield," Catania explained, flashing a smile at Mariposa.

"I see," the king said, scratching his chin. Then he leaned down and growled in Zee's face. *Grr!*

Zee raised her eyebrows. *Impressive!*

"Clearly I have much to learn about Butterfly Fairy customs. Shall we move to the ballroom for tea?" King Regellius asked. He offered his arm to escort Mariposa. "Madame Ambassador?"

Mariposa took his arm and shared a secret smile with Catania. The introductions hadn't gone exactly as planned, but at least she'd made a new friend.

Chapter 7

While Mariposa sat down to tea, Carlos was trying his best to fill her shoes at the royal library. He had promised Mariposa he would take his work seriously. He only wished he could say the same for Willa. She was late!

Carlos squatted down and heaved a heavy box of books into the air. The books were piled so high he could hardly see over the top. He bobbed and weaved through the bookcases, trying to find a place for them when—*crash!*— he ran smack into Willa.

Willa carried a paper bag and sipped a fairy smoothie, lost in her own thoughts. "Whoa- hoa! Hey, watch where you're going!" she cried, taking another sip of her drink. "You almost made me spill my smoothie!"

Carlos wobbled, trying to save his stack of books. But they tumbled out of his hands and all over the floor. He sighed. Filling Mariposa's shoes was hard work—especially with Willa around!

"Carlos!" Willa cried, recognizing him now that his face wasn't hidden behind books. "Good morning!"

Carlos rolled his eyes and knelt to pick up his spill. "It's afternoon, actually," he replied testily.

"Oops, I slept in," she said breezily. "Then I stopped by Flutter's Bakery for some Poof Pastries." She held up her paper bag. "Breaky?"

"It's lunchtime," Carlos snapped, hoisting the box once more.

"Harrumph. No breakfast for you, then," Willa huffed. She wondered what had made Carlos so grouchy today. *Library work must not agree with him,* she thought.

Carlos put his box down and picked up a nearby clipboard. "Now, let's see," he said, examining it. "Today's shipment of books has already come in. Check!" He looked down the list for the next item. "Inventory new books."

He gazed around the library floor at the piles of books and frowned. "Hmmm. This could take a while."

Willa sat down on a stack of boxes, bit into a pastry, and waved to Carlos.

Carlos shot her a look. It looked like it would take more than a while.

Mariposa set down her teacup and admired her surroundings. A huge, beautifully glowing Crystallite chandelier illuminated the ballroom. The king, the princess, Zee, and Anu were quietly sipping their tea as Talayla raced around refilling trays and cups. Sylvie, the princess's Pegasus, sat quietly in the corner.

Mariposa took a bite of her tea sandwich and let out a breath she hadn't realized she'd been holding. Maybe she was cut out for this ambassador stuff after all!

However, while she was starting to feel more comfortable with her role in Shimmervale, she was having a hard time getting used to how small everything was here. The Crystal Fairies had tinier wings than Butterfly Fairies—especially Mariposa's. She had to admit she felt a bit cramped at the table. Each time she reached for her teacup, she had to be careful not to knock anything—or anyone—over with her large, colorful wings. If only she had a bit more space!

". . . so to defeat the Skeezites," the king was saying, "your people must be trained as warriors from birth."

"What?" Mariposa replied, slightly shocked. She knew that in Flutterfield, Butterfly Fairies didn't know everything there was to know about Crystal Fairies. Still, she couldn't believe some of the strange stories floating around Shimmervale about Butterfly Fairies. "We're not warriors," she tried to explain. "I mean, we have warriors, but we're a very peaceful people." Out of the corner of her eye, she caught Zee throwing a scone at Anu. She shot her a look. *Not now!*

"More tea?" Talayla asked, hovering over her shoulder.

"Please," Mariposa replied, leaning to the

side to make room for Talayla to pour.

Talayla leaned toward her cup, but Mariposa's wings were just too big. She tried again as the king continued talking.

"But I was under the impression that Butterfly Fairies were built for battle. The laser vision, the claws, the fire breath!" he said.

"Fire breath? Um . . . we don't actually have any of those things." Mariposa exhaled. She tried to change the subject. "I love how the Crystallites shimmer in the sun." She reached out a hand to touch one.

"Don't touch that!" the king shouted. "The Crystallites are only to be touched by Crystal Fairies."

Mariposa shrank back in her chair. "Oh. Of course," she said softly.

"I'm sorry, if I could just—" Talayla whispered, still trying to refill Mariposa's teacup.

"Oh, excuse me. Here," Mariposa leaned all the way to one side, forgetting just for a second how big her wings were. They knocked over a crystal pitcher, sending a wave of water straight toward the king's robes. *Splash!*

"My word!" the king exclaimed, jumping from his chair just in time.

Mariposa covered her mouth with both hands. "Oh, no!" She wheeled around to apologize. *Bap!* Her wings smacked into Talayla, who spilled her pot of tea all over Zee.

"Aaaahhh!" Talayla cried.

Zee made a face and tried to shake the tea from her fur. *Yuck!* Then she tasted a bit of it and rubbed her belly. *Yum!* Chai was her favorite!

Mariposa used her napkin to sop up some of the water, but her wings were just too big to not be in the way. She knocked over a tray of sandwiches and sent Catania's muffin into her lap.

"I'm so sorry. . . . This is awful. . . . Let me help," Mariposa said.

"Here, let me," Catania offered, chuckling.

Mariposa gave her a grateful smile. "Thank you." But even her thank-you led to disaster as her wings toppled a tower of petit fours all over the king. "Did I get you? Let me see." She leaned toward him, but King Regellius put up his hands to stop her.

"Please," he barked sternly. "I'd rather you didn't." He took a deep breath to collect himself.

Mariposa felt herself turning red. This was a catastrophe!

"Perhaps, Madame Ambassador," the king began, "it would be best if you simply sat down and moved a bit farther back from the table."

"Of course, Your Majesty," Mariposa agreed, moving her chair a few feet away.

King Regellius waved his hand. "Perhaps a bit farther," he suggested.

Mariposa scooted back some more.

"A bit more . . . more. Teeny bit farther," the king continued as Mariposa kept sliding her chair. "Perfect!" he finally announced.

Mariposa fluttered her wings, giving them a good stretch. It felt nice to have enough space— even if she was nowhere near the table now.

Meanwhile, Zee and Anu had declared a food fight. Zee lobbed a mini muffin at Anu, who returned the favor by flicking cucumber slices at

Zee. Two of the slices hit Zee right in the eyes and stuck there. Zee shook them off and glared at Anu.

Anu looked around innocently, as if nothing had happened.

Zee put a petit four on her spoon and sent it spinning toward Anu slingshot-style—but it hit the king instead. *Whap!*

Anu giggled gleefully as the king's face turned red with rage.

Mariposa cringed.

"This royal tea is over!" the king thundered, pushing his chair back from the table. "Come, Catania!"

Catania and Mariposa exchanged worried glances. This was not how the afternoon was supposed to go!

As Mariposa slumped in her chair, Zee gave her an apologetic look. So much for good first impressions.

Chapter 8

That evening, in different section of Fairytopia, an evil fairy called Gwyllion was busy at work in a rustic cabin in the woods. The old crone, with wings like a dragonfly, leaned on her wooden staff. She bent over a ruby-red gemstone on a table.

Talking to her pet bat, she said, "Now is the time, Boris. Eight years of biding my time and planning my revenge. Eight years to hone my magic and become even more powerful."

Boris flapped his jet-black wings. "Has it been eight years already? Eight years of talk and no action. When are we going to get to the revenge?"

"Silence!" Gwyllion commanded. "I need to concentrate." She closed her eyes and hovered a wrinkled, knobby hand over the gemstone.

Deep in concentration, she tapped her staff twice on the ground, sending a shiver of black magic over the floor. The magic rippled up the table, which began to shake. It wrapped itself around the gemstone, cloaking it in blackness until it started to soak into the gem. The stone shivered, turning from a radiant red to a dull gray as the magic seeped inside.

Gwyllion opened her eyes and smiled a sinister smile. "Yes!" she cackled. "It's beautiful! Soon, all of Shimmervale's Crystallites will have had their final glow."

Gwyllion shuffled toward the fireplace. She peered into a cauldron, which bubbled over the fire and gave off green smoke. She plucked a jar from a nearby shelf and tossed a handful of blue powder into the cauldron. The green smoke rose and swirled high, slowly revealing an image from Shimmervale. It was King Regellius in his throne room late at night. He was gazing out the window at the moon, as if hoping it would tell him something. Gwyllion cackled gleefully as she watched Catania enter the room.

"Father?" Catania said.

King Regellius erased the worried look from his face and turned at the sound of his daughter's voice. "Catania. It's late. You should be in bed."

"I know," Catania replied. "For what it's worth, I don't think Mariposa means us any harm."

The king considered his daughter's words. "Perhaps. Perhaps not. I just hope she can help us."

Catania joined her father at the window, and they both looked up at the moon.

The scene over the cauldron grew fuzzy, and Gwyllion rubbed her gnarled hands together, plotting.

Chapter 9

Later that night, Mariposa used a Flutterlight to read in bed. Zee slept next to her, snoring softly. Mariposa envied the snoozing puffball—she hadn't been able to relax since their disastrous tea with the king. How had things started off so wonderfully, only to end in such a mess? Mariposa had unpacked all of her books on Shimmervale and set to studying. Maybe there was some crucial fact about the Crystal Fairies that she had missed—a key to making sure they saw her as a help and not a threat.

Zee rolled over and opened one eye.

"Can't sleep, Zee?" Mariposa asked.

Zee squinted at the light. *It's too bright in here!*

"I know," Mariposa replied, missing Zee's hint. "I couldn't sleep, either. I think I unintentionally insulted the king. I guess I don't know as much about Shimmervale as I thought." She hung her head.

Zee gave her a sympathetic pat and then rolled over grumpily.

Mariposa looked down at the book in her lap. "It says here that outsiders are forbidden to touch a Crystallite, especially the Heartstone, which is the most powerful Crystallite in Shimmervale. That's why the king was so upset at the tea."

Zee dramatically pulled her pillow over her head.

Mariposa chuckled. "Sorry, Zee, but I'm not tired . . . and this light just makes me feel like I'm at home."

Zee took the pillow off her head. She wished Mariposa wouldn't worry so much. She wondered if there was something she could do to take her mind off of things. Suddenly, she had it! Grinning mischievously, Zee picked up her pillow. *Whack!* She playfully hit Mariposa in the head with it.

Mariposa's mouth dropped open and she giggled. "Hey!" she cried, grabbing a pillow of her own.

Early the next morning, Mariposa heard a knock on her bedroom door.

"Huh?" She poked her head from under the covers and rubbed her eyes. It was still dark outside.

Talayla stuck her head in the door. "Ready for your introduction to the people of Shimmervale?" she asked perkily.

Mariposa groaned. What if she made another mess of things?

"We don't want to keep the king and princess waiting!" Talayla continued. "Not to mention an entire kingdom of Crystal Fairies!"

Mariposa yawned and stretched. Talayla was right. She shook Zee gently.

Zee let out a sleepy growl from under her pillow.

"Come on!" Mariposa urged.

As they flew from the palace into the city, Mariposa wondered how many Crystal Fairies would turn out to see her. She tried to ignore the nervous feeling in her stomach. Ahead of her, the king and princess rode in the royal carriage. It was decorated with warmly glowing Crystallites.

"Mariposa," the king called, motioning her to his side. "Before our conversation got, well, interrupted yesterday, you were about to enlighten me as to your weapons training and hand-to-hand combat skills."

"Combat skills?" Mariposa repeated.

"Yes, the ones you used to fight the Skeezites, of course."

"Oh," Mariposa began. She wrung her hands. As usual, the king had the wrong idea about her—about all Butterfly Fairies, really—but she wasn't sure how to tell him. "Well, it never really came down to 'battle.' Rayla, Rayna, and I met Zinzie, and then we all flew to the Bewilderness, where we found clues leading to the mermaids, who told us to fly east—"

The king waved his hand impatiently. "If you don't want to tell me, just say so!"

Mariposa sighed helplessly. How could she make him see the truth?

"Shimmervale City, Your Highnesses," Talayla announced, sweeping an arm toward the city.

Mariposa looked around. The streets were empty. Somewhere she heard a window slam shut.

"Please welcome Mariposa, our Royal Ambassador from Flutterfield," Talayla went on in her official voice.

Princess Catania looked around, surprised at the deserted city. "Well, it looks like everyone is busy today," she offered, smiling at Mariposa.

King Regellius furrowed his brow. "It appears my subjects are . . . preoccupied today."

"No, we're not!" cried a fairy from somewhere down the street.

Mariposa bit her lip. She felt her eyes well up with tears. She'd traveled all this way, and no one was interested in meeting her. How could she return to Flutterfield and report to

Queen Marabella that she had failed in her job as ambassador? She covered her face with her hands and turned to leave. As she did, her wings knocked the king's crown right off his head!

Somewhere, a fairy shouted, "She's attacking the king!"

"Butterfly Fairy attack!" cried another hidden Crystal Fairy.

Mariposa bent to retrieve the crown and stepped on the king's foot by mistake.

"Oof!" he grunted, stumbling forward.

Mariposa handed him his crown, noticing that it was bent at a funny angle. "I'm sorry! Your crown, Your Majesty!"

"Perhaps you beat the Skeezites by tripping over them," the king said meanly, flying away.

Catania watched him leave, looking concerned. She turned to Mariposa. "There will be more people here tomorrow. I'm sure of it," she offered.

"No, there won't!" cried another fairy.

Mariposa blew out a frustrated breath. If only she could believe Catania.

Back at the royal library, Carlos stood in front of a hanging tapestry. He delicately dabbed at some worn spots with his paintbrush, trying to restore the image on the fabric. He stepped back to admire his work.

"There we go. Almost finished," he said to himself. Then he heard Willa's voice in the distance. He looked over his shoulder to see Willa leading a group of fairy tourists toward the archives.

"We're flying. . . . We're flying . . . ," Willa announced in her best tour-guide voice. "And we're stopping."

She gestured for her small group of tourists to come in closer so they could hear her. She cleared her throat. "A long time ago—I forget how long—our fairy forefathers built Flutterfield on top of a putrid swamp."

One of the tourists raised his hand. "But, miss?" he asked, leafing through a brochure. "It says here that Flutterfield was built on a magnificent and exquisite garden."

Willa cocked her head to the side. *Hmm.* "Moving on," she announced, leading the group toward Carlos. "Okay, over here you'll see our resident mural . . . guy . . . painting some kind of picture."

The crowd marveled at his work.

"Willa!" Carlos exclaimed. "You're not supposed to bring visitors back here! Please stand back," he said, ushering the tourists away from the delicate tapestry. "This is very . . . fragile." He winced as someone bumped into his paint supply and sent paint splattering all over the tapestry.

Willa made a face. "Okay, people. We're flying. We're flying. . . ." She led the tourists out of the room as Carlos tried to clean the ruined tapestry. Being a tour guide was rough work! At the end of a long hallway, Willa continued, "Here you'll notice the royal lunchroom."

"You're not very good at this, are you?" one of the tourists asked.

"Can I get a refund?" asked another.

"When is Mariposa coming back?" inquired a third.

Not soon enough, Willa thought, blowing out a sigh.

Chapter 10

Mariposa yawned and stretched. Then, bubbling with excitement, she leaped out of bed. She'd spent much of the previous night reading up on Shimmervale, and she now felt certain that she could impress the Crystal Fairies. She bounded across the room and pounced on Zee, who was sleeping peacefully.

"Good morning, Zee!" she exclaimed.

Zee jumped out of bed and bumped her head on a tree-branch decoration. *Ahhhhh!*

"Today will be better, Zee. I just know it!"

Just then, there was a knock on their door.

Talayla breezed in, holding a dress.

"Good morning!" she sang, hanging the dress in the closet. "The king asked me to invite you to the annual Crystal Ball."

Mariposa is a Butterfly Fairy.
She lives in Flutterfield.

The queen of Flutterfield asks Mariposa to go
to Shimmervale as an ambassador.

Mariposa and her puffball friend Zee arrive
in Shimmervale.

Talayla shows Mariposa her new—
and strange—room.

Mariposa meets King Regellius and
Princess Catania.

Mariposa is sad when her meeting
with the king does not go as well as she hoped.

Mariposa and Catania have a wonderful day
together at Glow Water Falls.

Mariposa and Catania exchange gifts.
They will be friends forever!

The fairies have a blast dancing at the ball.

The king thinks Mariposa has stolen a Crystallite!
He orders her to leave Shimmervale.

On their way out of Shimmervale, Mariposa and Zee spot the evil Gwyllion!

Mariposa tells Catania that Gwyllion is trying to destroy Shimmervale. They have to stop her.

Oh, no! Evil magic freezes Mariposa when she tries to stop Gwyllion from destroying the powerful Heartstone.

Catania flies to the rescue!

Mariposa and Catania work together to bring the Heartstone back to life and save Shimmervale!

The fairies celebrate with a fabulous royal ball.

"Crystal Ball? What's that?" Mariposa asked.

"Just the biggest social event of the year!" Talayla replied. "Everyone comes to the palace to celebrate!"

Mariposa clapped her hands. "That's perfect! I'll win over the citizens of Shimmervale, and the king will see that we can all get along." She turned to Talayla. "Do you know where I can find him? I want to thank him for the invitation."

A short while later, Mariposa and Zee flew down a long hallway toward the palace library. Mariposa knocked lightly on the door. Too eager, she entered without waiting for an answer.

Inside, she saw the king hovering over a scale model of Shimmervale. He seemed to be moving small army fairies into various positions on a battlefield. Catania was reading by the window with Anu on her lap.

"Now, where is my third flying battalion?" the king said to himself.

Mariposa realized that neither the king nor the princess had heard her and Zee come in.

"When you're responsible for the kingdom, Catania," the king continued, deep in thought, "it will be important that you place your guards at all the strategic locations from which an enemy could attack."

Catania turned the page of her book. "Oh, yes. Mmm-hmm," she said, but she was more interested in reading her story.

Mariposa cleared her throat. "Your Majesty," she called.

The king gave a small jump and looked up, annoyed.

Anu spied Zee and picked up one of the king's figurines, preparing to launch it.

"Your Majesty," Mariposa continued, "thank you for the invitation; I'm very honored. I wanted to know if you want me to, well, address your subjects at the ball. I bring greetings from Queen Marabella, and I could simply say that everyone in Flutterfield sends their good wishes."

The king put a finger to his chin. He spent a

few moments considering Mariposa's proposal.

She crossed her fingers, hoping he liked her idea.

"Let's see how it goes at the ball, Mariposa," the king replied carefully. "And perhaps you can address the people."

Mariposa twirled around, delighted. "Thank you, Your Majesty!" she cried.

Anu sent his figurine flying across the room, hitting Zee square on the behind.

"Oww!" Zee yelped, and bumped into a tall lamp. The lamp wobbled, teetering back and forth, until finally it fell—right into the king's model battlefield!

"Zee, no!" Mariposa cried. She rushed to try to catch the pieces, but instead, her wings sent more pieces to the floor.

King Regellius's face turned red with rage. "Look what you've done!" he thundered.

"I'm so sorry. Here, let me help you pick up the pieces," Mariposa said, kneeling on the floor.

"Father, it was an accident," Catania said.

But the king wasn't listening. He turned to

Mariposa. "Honestly, I'm not even sure why I agreed to this arrangement. And those wings! They're a menace! Can't you do anything about them?"

Mariposa was confused. Her wings were a part of her. She couldn't just make them disappear. "*Do* anything? Um, well, I guess I . . ." She struggled to think of some way to make her wings smaller. Finally, she managed to fold them down and around her like a skirt.

King Regellius nodded. "Better. Keep them that way," he ordered as he strode out of the room.

Catania gave Mariposa an apologetic look. "I'm sorry. It's just he— I'll talk to him," she promised, hopping on Sylvie the Pegasus. "Father!" she called. And Sylvie took flight.

Mariposa watched them leave the room and then looked down at her wing skirt. It was so uncomfortable!

"Keep them this way?" she said.

As if they'd heard her, Mariposa's wings sprang back open on their own. They knocked

Zee right in the face with a thud.

"That could be difficult." Mariposa hung her head.

Later that day, Mariposa sat outside on a balcony, hugging her knees. She couldn't understand how so much had gone so wrong! All she had wanted was to explain to the citizens of Shimmervale how much the citizens of Flutterfield wanted to be friends. And yet, every time she tried, disaster occurred. Queen Marabella was going to be so disappointed. Mariposa sighed.

Just then, Zee flew up with a bouquet of Shimmervale flowers.

"Thank you, Zee," Mariposa said, smiling sadly. She stuck her nose into the bouquet and took a big sniff. Seconds later, she began to sneeze. *Achoo! Achoo! Achoo!*

Zee grabbed the bouquet and tossed it aside. She was trying to help Mariposa feel better, but so far, she'd caused nothing but trouble.

Across Fairytopia, Gwyllion stood over her cauldron once more, Boris on her shoulder.

As her magic smoke rose, it revealed an image of King Regellius on his throne. She watched as the door opened and Talayla entered.

"You wanted to see me, Your Majesty?" Talayla asked.

King Regellius beckoned for her to come closer. "I want you to stay close to Mariposa at the ball, Talayla. It's our most important celebration, and I don't want anything to go wrong."

Talayla nodded seriously. "Yes, sir."

The image faded and Gwyllion cackled evilly. Her plan was coming together!

"You see, Boris?" she said. "Patience is a virtue. Everyone in Shimmervale, all in one place. Sharpen your talons, my friend. We go tonight."

Boris rubbed his wings together and moved toward the sharpening stone. He ran his talons along the stone, sparks flying left and right.

Gwyllion smiled and patted her wicked little bat on the head.

Tonight would be the night. Shimmervale, beware.

Chapter 11

That afternoon, Mariposa made her way back to her room, trying to keep her wings folded down as the king had instructed. But it was no use. Sproing! They shot up again, smacking Zee. Mariposa winced. Just one more disaster! "Sorry," she said sadly.

She reached her room and opened the door. When she looked inside, her jaw dropped.

Her bedroom had been completely transformed! The scary branches and evil-looking tree villains were gone. They had been replaced by beautiful flowers and bright colors. It looked just like the Flutterfield home that Mariposa knew and loved—and missed. But how had this happened?

Just then, Catania popped her head in the

door. "Did I get it right?" she asked.

"*You* did this?" Mariposa was almost too stunned to speak.

Catania nodded. "You worked so hard to learn about us, the least we could do is return the favor. Is it anything like home?"

Mariposa admired the plush, cozy seating and the warm afternoon light streaming through the windows. "Almost exactly!" she exclaimed.

Catania beamed. "I've actually been reading up on Flutterfield since I found out you were coming," she admitted proudly.

"You have?"

"I love to read," Catania explained. "Sometimes I feel like I never want to leave the palace; I'm perfectly happy spending the whole day lost in books."

Mariposa couldn't believe her ears. It sounded just like someone else she knew. "Me too!" she cried excitedly.

"I've noticed," Catania replied. "That's why I think you'll like this."

She turned toward Anu, who was battling

Zee for a spot on a flower hammock. "Anu?"

Hearing his name called, Anu reluctantly let Zee stretch out on the hammock. He flew toward the wall and pulled a cord on the side.

A pair of flowing, gauzy drapes opened, and Mariposa gasped. Behind the curtain stood a bookcase chock-full of books! "Catania! You did this, too?"

"Well, I had some help," Catania said, winking at Anu.

Mariposa flew up and down the wall of books, inspecting them. "This is incredible!" She pointed to a thick volume on a shelf. "I can't believe it—have you read this, *Flight of Fancy*? It's one of my all-time favorites!"

Catania put a hand on her chest. "Mine too!" She thought for a moment and then said, "Grab it. I want to show you something." She raced to the open French doors in the room and whistled. A minute later, Sylvie landed on the balcony.

Sylvie looked at Mariposa and then at Catania. She cocked her head with concern.

"It's okay, Sylvie. We can trust Mariposa." She

climbed on Sylvie's back and called to Mariposa over her shoulder. "Follow us!"

Sylvie fluttered effortlessly into the air.

Anu, fighting once more with Zee over the hammock, saw that Catania was leaving. He gave Zee a final swinging shove in the hammock and flew out the window.

"Ahh!" Zee cried as she spun.

Mariposa untangled Zee, and they followed Catania, Sylvie, and Anu up, up, up toward the roof of the palace. They landed on top of a huge spire, and Mariposa looked around at a lush rooftop garden. The space was covered with beautiful green plants and cushy places to sit. On the next level up, she noticed the biggest Crystallite she'd ever seen.

"This is my favorite place to read," Catania explained.

"It's perfect," Mariposa replied.

"You can see all the way to the Palian Sea from there," the princess declared, pointing to the higher level. "Come on up."

Mariposa hesitated. "But isn't that a

Crystallite?" After what the king had told her, she wasn't sure she should fly anywhere near it.

"Only the most important one in all the land—come on!" said Catania.

Warily, Mariposa followed Catania and Sylvie up to the very tallest spire of the palace. "This is the Heartstone, isn't it?" she asked, careful not to fly too close.

"Yes," Catania confirmed. "It's the most powerful Crystallite we have. I feel safe when I'm near it. Like nothing can harm me."

Mariposa's ears pricked up. "Harm you? Who would want to harm you?"

Catania looked uncomfortable. "Er . . . ," she began. Then she changed the subject. "It must be hard being away from Flutterfield. Do you miss it?"

Mariposa furrowed her brow. "I miss Flutterfield a little," she answered, "but I'm really enjoying getting to explore Shimmervale." She took in the gorgeous view around her. "I can't wait to see Glow Water Falls again."

"I haven't been there in years," Catania said.

"You're kidding. Years?" Mariposa couldn't believe it. If Flutterfield had something as spectacular as Glow Water Falls, she'd be there all the time!

"Since I was eight," Catania said.

"Why not?" Mariposa asked. It didn't make sense.

"I don't know," the princess replied, looking down.

Mariposa looked in the direction of the Falls and back to Catania, who was lost in her own thoughts. "Let's go now," Mariposa suggested.

"Now?" Catania looked frightened.

"It'll be an adventure," Mariposa declared.

"I'm really not up for an adventure."

"Okay, not an adventure. An excursion! You just said you haven't been there in years. Don't you miss it?" Mariposa asked.

"A lot," Catania admitted. "But the Crystal Ball is this afternoon. We should get ready."

"It'll be quick," Mariposa pressed. "We'll be back in two wing flaps."

Catania bit her lip in thought. "Okay, just for

a little bit," she said uncertainly.

Sylvie let out a loud, concerned neigh.

Catania patted her mane. "I understand, Sylvie. It'll be okay, though. We can trust them. They're our friends."

Sylvie frowned, unconvinced. But she bent so that Catania could climb aboard her back easily, and the fairies flew off to the Falls, with Zee and Anu trailing behind them.

Chapter 12

"Woo-hoo!" Mariposa cried with delight as they glided over Glow Water Falls.

"You think *this* is amazing?" Catania called from Sylvie's back. "Follow me!"

The girls swooped down and landed on the bank at the bottom of the Falls.

"You're right!" Mariposa said, grinning. She gazed around the beautiful little cove where they stood. Colorful, glowing Crystallites nestled at the base of the gushing rainbow falls. It was stunning!

Mariposa watched as Catania admired their surroundings. It was almost as if the princess was seeing it all for the first time. Catania bent down and picked up a handful of pebble-sized Crystallites. They glowed softly in her hand.

"Have you ever skipped Rainbow Rocks?" she asked Mariposa.

"How would I have ever skipped Rainbow Rocks?" Mariposa said, laughing.

Catania grinned and tossed one toward the water. It skidded across the surface—one, two, three, four. But the best part was that as it skipped it chimed music! "You try!" Catania said, handing Mariposa a rock.

Mariposa gave it her best toss. One, two, three, four, five! "Woo-hoo!" she yelped.

The girls continued skipping stones, making an upbeat tune as each rock hit the water. Anu and Zee couldn't help themselves and started dancing right along with the music. Catania nudged Mariposa to take a look, and the four friends dissolved into giggles.

When they had finished skipping Rainbow Rocks, Mariposa and Catania sat back to back, reading books contentedly. Zee and Anu made silly faces in the water's reflection.

"I've missed this place," Catania admitted, closing her book.

Mariposa turned to look at her friend. "Why has it been so long?"

Catania paused. She looked unsure how to explain.

"Does it have anything to do with why you don't fly?" Mariposa asked gently.

Catania looked surprised. "What do you mean?"

"Well," Mariposa began, "Sylvie flies you everywhere, even when you're inside the castle."

Catania folded her arms across her chest. "Maybe that's because I'm a princess. I don't have to fly if I don't want to. It's my privilege," she said unconvincingly.

"Maybe . . . but that doesn't sound like you," replied Mariposa.

Catania looked guilty.

"It's okay. You don't have to talk about it if you don't want to," Mariposa assured her. She didn't want her new friend to feel uncomfortable.

"No, I do want to talk about it," Catania said.

Mariposa noticed Anu and Sylvie exchange a concerned look.

"I was eight years old," Catania began. "My father and I were having a picnic at the top of these very falls when suddenly, we saw something below."

Mariposa nodded to show she was listening carefully.

"It was an old woman," Catania continued. "She wasn't from Shimmervale, but she and her pet bat were poking around the Crystallites.

"My father confronted the woman, and she asked for a Crystallite. I knew what my father would say. He told me all the time: Our responsibility is to the Crystal Fairies. If we let other creatures have Crystallites, we could end up without enough for our own subjects," Catania recalled.

"So your father said no," Mariposa guessed.

Catania nodded.

"What did the old woman do?" Mariposa asked.

"She wasn't happy," Catania explained. She stared into the distance, remembering.

"You dare deny Gwyllion?" the old woman shouted at the king.

Catania watched from the top of the Falls as her father tried to reason with Gwyllion. But it was too late. The old woman banged her walking staff on the ground twice. *Boom! Boom!*

Horrified, Catania watched as a wave of magic rushed from the stick and spread along the ground. It raced right to the king's feet and snaked up his legs, freezing him on the spot.

"I . . . can't . . . move!" the king cried, terrified.

"You had your chance," Gwyllion growled, walking toward him. "Now you owe me *all* your Crystallites."

"Noooo!" Catania cried from the hilltop, flying toward the old woman. She couldn't let Gwyllion take her father away.

"Catania! Get back!" the king pleaded.

But Catania wouldn't listen.

Gwyllion gave a wicked smile as she watched Catania soar toward them. She shot a blast of magic right toward Catania. It froze her in midair and then—just as quickly—she was falling!

Gwyllion leaped into the air and caught Catania with one arm a split second before she hit the ground.

Catania worked to free herself, but the old woman was surprisingly strong.

"Say good-bye to your little one!" Gwyllion bellowed to the king with an evil laugh.

The king struggled with all his might against the magic that had frozen him. Finally, he was able to break free! He lunged toward Gwyllion.

Gwyllion looked over her shoulder in time to see the king racing right for her.

"Give me back my daughter!" the king ordered, grabbing on to Gwyllion's ankles.

But Gwyllion stood firm. "No!"

The king swung his body around and kicked her magic walking stick, breaking it in two. *Crack!* The sound echoed off the nearby Falls.

"My staff!" Gwyllion cried. She watched the two pieces of her precious staff plummet toward the ground; then she tossed Catania into the air.

"Daddy!" Catania screamed. The king raced across the ground and put out his arms to catch her. But he wasn't fast enough.

"You treat me with this disrespect?" Gwyllion cried, soaring into the sky above. "You will regret this!"

But the king hardly noticed her leave as he cradled an unconscious Catania in his arms.

Catania shook her head, as if sweeping the memory out of her mind. "Both my wings were broken. They healed, but I haven't flown since," she said softly.

"What happened to Gwyllion?" Mariposa asked.

Catania shrugged. "She never came back."

Mariposa put a hand on her friend's shoulder. "Are you worried she will?"

"My father worries about it a lot," Catania answered. "It's the real reason he allowed you to come."

Mariposa nodded. Finally, she understood

the real reason she was in Shimmervale. "So the king wants advice on fighting Gwyllion," she said. "But he could have just asked Queen Marabella. I'm sure she would have—"

Catania shook her head. "No. He doesn't trust Butterfly Fairies enough for that."

Mariposa frowned. "Do you?"

"Yes. Which is why I want you to have this." Catania pulled a necklace from her skirt pocket. Dangling from the chain was a Crystallite that matched her own necklace. Catania held it out to Mariposa.

Mariposa was touched. But considering the king's rules about Crystallites, she wasn't sure she could accept Catania's offering. "Catania, I can't," she answered awkwardly. "With our history, no Butterfly Fairy should ever take a Crystallite from Shimmervale."

"You're not taking it," Catania insisted. "It's a gift."

Mariposa smiled and fastened the beautiful necklace around her neck, grateful to be making a new friend. She thought for a moment and then smiled. "I have something for you, too," she said, pulling the Flutter Flower from her satchel. It glowed softly in her hands.

"It's so pretty!" Catania exclaimed.

"It's a Flutter Flower," explained Mariposa. "I thought I needed it to remind me of home. Maybe after I leave, it can remind you of me."

"Thank you!" Catania cried.

The two girls admired their gifts and smiled at one another. Then, as if by magic, the flower and the necklace began to glow strongly.

"Whoa!" the fairies both cried, delighted.

Mariposa couldn't remember the last time she felt this happy. There was nothing like the glow of true friendship, she thought.

Suddenly, Sylvie began neighing loudly.

Catania looked at her, puzzled, and then slapped her forehead. "The Crystal Ball! We need to get ready!"

The girls tucked their gifts safely beneath their shirts and took off for the palace.

Chapter 13

In Flutterfield, the sun shone high in the midday sky. Carlos sealed a box and placed it on top of a heap of identical boxes. He leaned against the stack and wiped his brow.

Willa fluttered in and gave an exhausted sigh. "My wings feel like they've been flapping for days," she said.

Carlos nodded. "It's been a long week. But I think we did it."

Willa looked around and nodded proudly. "I think you're right. Mariposa is gonna be so impressed. This wasn't so hard."

Carlos raised an eyebrow at her. Then he asked, "How did reading to the elderly go?"

"How am I supposed to know?" Willa asked. "I thought you were doing it?"

Carlos shook his head.

"Oh, no!" they both cried, and zipped out of the room.

Mariposa looked at herself one last time in the bedroom mirror. Her elegant pink-and-orange gown fit perfectly! Now if only she could keep her wings folded down in skirt position, the evening might be a success. She grabbed her *Shimmervale: A History* book for some last-minute studying.

"Listen to this, Zee," she said. "'At the Crystal Ball, Shimmervale fairies dance in unique aerial patterns.'" She looked up to make sure Zee was listening. Instead, she found the puffball staring at herself in the mirror.

Zee preened and batted her eyelashes. *How do I look?*

Mariposa laughed. Covered head to toe in bows, beads, and ribbons, Zee looked like a snowstorm of accessories!

Just then, they heard a knock on the door.

"Come in!" Mariposa called.

Talayla breezed into the room. She took one look at Mariposa and stopped in her tracks. "Oh, no!" she cried, distraught.

"What's wrong?" Mariposa asked.

Talayla shook her head with worry. "I came to get you for the ball, and you're not even ready!"

Mariposa looked down at her dress, confused. She twirled for Talayla. "Sure I am!"

"But you're not beshimmered!" Talayla moaned. She floated to the doorway and whistled loudly down the hall.

A moment later, three tiny shimmer fairies appeared. They moved in a cloud of sparkles and spoke in high-pitched voices. They zoomed over Mariposa's head and began to shimmy and dance, sending a shower of sparkles over her body and dress.

Mariposa giggled. "We do this in Flutterfield, too, only we call it befluttering!"

Next, the shimmer fairies began working on Zee. They sprinkled her with so many sparkles that she sneezed. *Achoo!*

Once Zee was beshimmered to their satisfaction, the shimmer fairies waved and zipped out of the room. They were gone as quickly as they had arrived.

Mariposa carefully folded her wings back down into a skirt and gave a final twirl. "What do you think now?" she asked Talayla.

Talayla looked puzzled. She had never seen Mariposa fold her wings before. She moved closer to examine the look. "Wow. . . . How did you—"

Sproing!

"Ahhh!" Talayla cried, jumping back just as Mariposa's wings popped open.

Mariposa winced. "It's not easy," she admitted. "I'll work on it on the way to the Crystal Ball."

A few minutes later, Mariposa took a deep breath as Talayla opened the ballroom door for her and Zee. This was it! She carefully folded her wings down one more time and floated into the ballroom.

The grand room glittered and glowed with the hustle and bustle of a party. Everywhere Mariposa looked, she saw beshimmered Crystal Fairies in gorgeous twinkling ball gowns. Waiters in bow ties flew around offering refreshments, and a band played upbeat music. It was the most beautiful party Mariposa had ever attended! She glided into the room, Talayla and Zee following behind, and looked around for Catania.

Suddenly, the princess swooped down next to them, riding in a sparkling sky-blue chariot pulled by Sylvie.

"Your wings!" Mariposa cried, noticing Catania's wings tucked tight around her waist like a peplum for her dress.

"If you have to fold down your wings, I will, too." She twirled to show off her wing skirt. "What do you think?"

"Beautiful," Mariposa replied. She was touched that Catania would go to such lengths to make sure she felt comfortable at such a big, important event. "Thank you."

"My pleasure, Your Ambassadress," the

princess replied. She bent to curtsy, but as soon as she did, her wings sprang up. "Oops. I'm still working on that."

Mariposa laughed, and the two friends moved through the ballroom.

"Just an intimate gathering with a couple of close friends?" Mariposa observed jokingly.

"I told you," Catania said. "*Everyone* comes to the Crystal Ball. I'd be surprised if anyone *isn't* here." The princess looked around at all the dancers flying and floating in the air and suddenly seemed sad.

"What is it?" Mariposa asked, noticing the frown on Catania's face.

Catania tried to laugh it off. "Nothing. It's just, I always loved dancing, until . . ." She trailed off.

But Mariposa knew what she meant. "Want to dance?" she asked, eyeing the floor below them.

"But I don't—"

"Sure you do," Mariposa insisted. "Sylvie, would you mind taking us down?"

Sylvie steered the chariot to the ground and came to a stop in front of the band.

Mariposa jumped out and immediately started twirling to the sound of the music, her feet firmly planted on the floor. A fairy didn't need to fly to shake and move!

Catania looked around, self-conscious. "But we're the only ones down here. What if everyone stares?"

"What if they do? Come on—it's fun!" Mariposa urged.

Just then, Mariposa's wings shot up. *Sproing!* Catania laughed so hard that hers sprang open, too. *Sproing!* The girls kept laughing and started to dance.

"You're right—this *is* fun!" Catania called over the thump of the drums.

"Told you!" Mariposa grinned.

The girls continued spinning and shimmying, and soon the fairies flying above them began to notice.

Zee and Anu flew down and started dancing the tango around them. Zee even had a flower in her mouth to really look the part. Then Talayla joined in, nudging her group of friends to come with her. Pretty soon the dance floor was swirling with Crystal Fairies of all kinds swaying and moving to the beat.

Catania and Mariposa were dancing in the middle of the crowd, arms linked and laughing, when King Regellius soared down to the dance floor.

"Having a good time?" he asked, startling the girls.

"Your Majesty!" exclaimed Mariposa.

"Father!" said Catania. She curtsyed and her wings sprang into Mariposa's, knocking her down. "Oh, no!"

But Mariposa laughed good-naturedly. "It's fine—now I know how it feels!"

As Catania helped Mariposa to her feet, neither girl noticed that Mariposa's Crystallite necklace had fallen out of her dress.

One of the Crystal Fairies nearby saw it and pointed a finger. "That Butterfly Fairy has a Crystallite!" A buzz traveled through the crowd as everyone found out about Mariposa's Crystallite.

"She must have *stolen* it!" accused another Crystal Fairy.

"I knew we couldn't trust them!" shouted a third.

"Look out for her laser vision!" The crowd started to panic, running in every direction.

King Regellius raised his hands. "Enough!" he thundered, silencing the crowd.

Everyone froze in their places. Anu even froze while dipping Zee.

The king turned to Mariposa. "Mariposa," he said seriously. "You stole a Crystallite, after we welcomed you. And trusted you."

Mariposa shook her head. "No, Your Majesty."

Catania stepped forward. "I *gave* it to her!" Catania explained. "We were at Glow Water Falls earlier, and—"

King Regellius held up a hand to silence her. "You went to Glow Water Falls *unprotected?*" he roared.

Catania cowered. "Mari-Mariposa and I—"

she stammered.

The king did not wait for her to finish. "Mariposa took you to Glow Water Falls? She's a Butterfly Fairy and in no position to know what's best for a Crystal Fairy princess!"

Mariposa stepped forward to explain. "We weren't doing anything wrong. I know why you're so protective, but—"

King Regellius turned red with rage. "You know *nothing*! You don't know what it's like to be responsible for a kingdom. You don't know how to protect us, so we have to protect ourselves." He pointed toward the door. "Leave! Immediately!"

"Leave . . . the ballroom?" Mariposa asked, stunned. Only moments ago they'd been dancing happily. How had things gone so wrong?

"Leave Shimmervale!" the king commanded. "And never come back!"

"Father—" Catania pleaded.

"Not now, Catania," the king snapped, still glaring at Mariposa.

"As you wish, Your Majesty," Mariposa

replied, handing the Crystallite necklace back to Catania. She fluttered toward the door, her wings wilted. Zee gave Anu a sad wave and rushed after Mariposa.

As they closed the door gently behind them, they could hear Catania still trying to explain.

"But, Father, I gave it to her!" Catania cried.

"Even more reason to separate you from an obviously bad influence," King Regellius announced.

Catania stomped her foot, then whistled for Sylvie, leaped on her back, and took off, Anu racing after her.

Chapter 14

Mariposa burst through the palace doors into the fresh air. She flew as fast as her wings could take her away from the king, Catania, and anything having to do with Crystallites. Zee struggled to keep up.

Once she was far enough away, Mariposa stopped to catch her breath. She looked back at the palace in the distance. It was beautiful, even if it did not welcome her anymore. She struggled to fight the tears welling in her eyes.

Zee rubbed Mariposa's back to comfort her.

"I don't know what's worse," Mariposa began, "that I failed, or that I have to go home and admit it to people who believed in me." She shook her head miserably.

Then, out of the corner of her eye, Mariposa

saw something dark moving through the clouds. It didn't look like any kind of fairy she'd ever seen. Something resembling a large bird or bat glided in the sky above it.

"What is that?" Mariposa wondered aloud to Zee.

She flew a little closer, careful to stay hidden behind plants and trees. She peeked over a bush and realized that the dark figure was an old woman stooped over some sort of walking stick. A large bat landed on her shoulder.

"I thought everyone was already at the ball," Mariposa said to Zee.

Zee nodded and started to fly away, but Mariposa pulled her back.

"We can't just go," Mariposa declared. "What if it's someone dangerous? What if—" Suddenly, she knew. "What if it's Gwyllion?"

Zee shrugged and tried to look concerned.

"Zee!" Mariposa cried, frustrated. "I know the king told us to leave, but we *have* to warn them!"

Zee looked unconvinced.

"We have to help the Crystal Fairies," said Mariposa. "They're our friends."

The puffball shook her head.

"Catania's our friend," Mariposa pressed. "And Sylvie. Are you going to tell me Anu isn't your friend?"

Zee blushed.

"And if the king and the other Crystal Fairies aren't our friends now—well, I'm going to be a friend to them when they need one most," she declared. She spun around and started back toward the palace.

Zee hesitated and then hurried after Mariposa.

As the sun sank behind Glow Water Falls, Mariposa and Zee peeked from behind a large rock. They eyed Gwyllion suspiciously.

She had landed on top of one of Shimmervale's tallest city buildings and was scanning the horizon. She watched the late-afternoon sun glint off the many different-colored Crystallites and smiled sinisterly. Then the old crone banged her staff on the rooftop twice. *Boom! Boom!*

Pea-green tendrils of magic swirled around Gwyllion and then snaked out over the city like lava. They slithered over each building, extinguishing Crystallites. One by one, the glowing stones turned dull and lifeless, like lumps of coal.

"I'll turn all the Crystallites to stone!" Gwyllion cackled.

"You're so wicked," said her sidekick, Boris, with an evil laugh.

Gwyllion pounded her staff again, and the green magic swept down and around Glow Water Falls, running over its Crystallites.

Mariposa and Zee watched in horror as, one by one, all of Shimmervale's Crystallites turned to stone.

Back at the palace, Catania sat in her favorite reading spot on the roof. But it was no use trying to concentrate. She could still hear the music from the Crystal Ball softly in the background. "I don't understand?" she said to Anu for the tenth time. "*He's* the one who doesn't understand!"

Anu looked at her sympathetically. He didn't know what to say. He'd never seen the king and the princess fight before.

Suddenly, Catania and Anu felt the ground rumble beneath them. They exchanged a worried look. What could that be?

The princess peered over the side of the turret and then dove for cover. Gwyllion was down below! Gathering her courage, Catania peeked once again over the palace wall. She watched as the old woman banged her staff on the ground twice, sending a dismal green magic toward the palace. It crept closer and closer and then began to climb up the palace walls.

"Oh, no!" Catania cried in horror. She whistled for Sylvie and together they raced toward the ballroom to warn everyone, but when she reached the ballroom windows, Anu tugged on her sleeve. He pointed to the magic that was already swirling under the door. He was trying to tell her that it wasn't safe to go inside.

Catania could hear frightened voices coming from the ballroom. She pressed her face to the glass to see what was happening.

Everyone was completely frozen. Gwyllion must have used the same horrible spell that she had cast on the king eight years before. Catania wasn't sure what to do. Then she heard someone calling for her.

"Catania!"

"Mariposa!" the princess cried in relief, recognizing her friend's voice.

"I think it's Gwyllion," Mariposa said. "She's putting out all the Crystallites!"

Catania nodded. "If she turns all the Crystallites to rock, Shimmervale will freeze!" she explained.

They heard panicked voices coming from the ballroom.

"I can't move!"

"Help!"

The girls watched as the magic climbed

higher and higher, threatening to engulf the entire palace.

"Father!" Catania shouted. She jumped on Sylvie and rode to another window to get a better look.

Mariposa followed, with Zee and Anu trailing behind.

The friends ducked behind a wall as Gwyllion came nearer. They watched as she and Boris flew into the ballroom. Catania led the way back to the window and held up her hand.

"Whatever we do, we can't touch that," she said, pointing to the green magic swirling inside the ballroom.

They pressed their faces to the glass once again and saw Gwyllion approaching the king. They could just make out the conversation.

"Gwyllion," the king growled.

"One Crystallite. That's all it would have taken," the old crone said.

"Stop, Gwyllion. Have mercy on us," the king pleaded, watching the smoking magic grow thicker and heavier.

"Yes," Gwyllion hissed. "I will show you the same mercy you showed me. Now watch as I destroy your most precious stone of all."

Mariposa saw Catania's face turn white.

"The Heartstone!" the princess cried. "The Heartstone is like a candle: if we keep it lit, we can relight all the other Crystallites."

Inside, Gwyllion laughed cruelly and, with one sweep of her staff, extinguished every Crystallite in the room. Then she flew out an open window.

"She's flying toward the Heartstone!" cried Catania.

Mariposa sprang into action. "We have to do what your father did," she said. "We find a way to break her magic staff."

Together, they set out for the rooftop where the Heartstone was kept.

Chapter 15

On the roof, Mariposa, Catania, Sylvie, Zee, and Anu were in view of the Heartstone. Zee gave Mariposa a questioning look. *Now what?*

"Now we stay very quiet . . . and wait," Mariposa commanded.

"And when we see Gwyllion?" Catania prodded, her voice shaking with fear.

Mariposa bit her lip. Gwyllion would arrive any minute, and then—well, she wasn't exactly sure what would happen then. She just knew that they couldn't let the Heartstone go dark without a fight.

The friends huddled together to stay warm against the frigid magic swirling around them.

Suddenly, Zee jumped and let out a squeal. She looked around frantically, as though she had heard something. *What was that?*

"Zee," Mariposa whispered. "You have to be very quiet."

Just then, Boris nose-dived toward the princess, knocking her over the ledge.

"Ahh!" cried Catania.

Sylvie plunged to catch her, but Boris attacked again, this time aiming his razor-sharp talons right at Sylvie's wings.

"Sylvie!" Catania cried as her beloved Pegasus neighed in pain.

Sylvie landed roughly on a nearby spire, Catania still on her back.

Mariposa, Zee, and Anu raced to Sylvie's side and prepared to defend her against Boris's next attack.

The bat dove at them again, but this time Anu and Zee pelted him with fruit from the roof garden. *Zing! Zap! Squish!*

Following their lead, Mariposa grabbed a giant fruit bowl. As Boris plummeted toward them once again, she slammed the bowl down on top of him, trapping him underneath. *Whump!*

Mariposa wiped her brow and took a deep breath. "Are you all right?" she asked Catania.

"I am," the princess replied, shaken. "But Sylvie's wing is hurt." She jumped off the Pegasus's back to inspect her injury.

Sylvie neighed softly and nuzzled Catania.

"She'll be okay. She just can't fly," the princess declared.

They heard a low evil laugh and looked into the sky. Gwyllion was racing toward the Heartstone with Boris right behind her!

"Oh, no!" Mariposa cried. The evil bat must have escaped while they were checking on Sylvie.

"For your selfishness, I will leave you with nothing!" Gwyllion's voice rang out.

Without hesitating, Mariposa rose into the air and dashed after Gwyllion. They had to save the Heartstone! She looked behind her to see Catania still on the rooftop. "Come fly with me!" she said.

But Catania looked terrified. "I can't. I don't fly . . . and it's Gwyllion. . . ."

Mariposa flew down to her friend and looked

her in the eyes. "You can do this, Catania. Be brave."

The princess shook her head. "I'm not brave. I'm scared. I can't."

Mariposa frowned. If only she could make Catania understand that she could do anything she put her mind to. But there was no time. "Stay here," she commanded, and took off toward the Heartstone.

Zee raced to follow Mariposa but stopped in her tracks. She gestured to Anu. *You coming?*

Anu looked questioningly at Catania.

The princess waved him away. "Of course. Go. Thank you," she told him.

The two puffballs joined hands and hurried after Mariposa.

Catania buried her face in her hands.

Moments later, Gwyllion closed her eyes and aimed her staff toward the Heartstone. She focused all her attention on it, willing her spell to work on such a large Crystallite.

"I can feel it," she murmured to Boris. "Not too much longer."

Just then, Mariposa rushed toward the Heartstone. "Gwyllion! Stop!"

Ahhh! Anu and Zee screamed to throw off the old crone's concentration. Gwyllion roared in frustration.

"Boris! Get her!" she commanded, pointing to Mariposa.

As Boris dove toward Mariposa, Zee and Anu lunged for Gwyllion's staff.

But Boris circled back around and chased them away. "Nice try, puffballs!" Then he plunged toward them. "Yum, dinner!"

The puffballs glided higher into the air, locked in a high-stakes game of chase with the evil bat.

Meanwhile, Gwyllion was concentrating all of her energy on the Heartstone once again. She pounded her staff on the ground twice. *Boom! Boom!*

Mariposa hid behind a nearby spire. She waited until Gwyllion was totally focused on her spell. Ready . . . set . . . go time! She lunged toward the evil woman, reaching for the staff.

But Gwyllion must have sensed the attack. At the last second, she spun around and shot a blast of powerful magic right at Mariposa.

"Ahhhhh!" Mariposa wailed as the green magic surrounded her. She landed hard on the rooftop, frozen stiff.

At the same time, Boris dive-bombed Anu and Zee, sending them into Mariposa's green cloud. They turned into Puffball Popsicles!

Gwyllion laughed with delight. She focused on the Heartstone, which was starting to flicker. "It's happening! It's happening!" She tightened her grip on her staff, and the mighty Crystallite flickered again.

Mariposa struggled against the evil woman's spell, but she was no match for Gwyllion's magic. Mariposa watched helplessly as the very heart of Shimmervale burnt out right before her eyes.

Chapter 16

Suddenly, Catania flew out of the shadows! "Nooo!" she screamed, diving right toward Gwyllion.

Mariposa turned to see Catania soaring toward them. *She's flying!* Mariposa thought excitedly. Mariposa's heart soared. "Catania!" she shouted.

Catania slammed into Gwyllion, knocking her off her feet. As she fell, Gwyllion lost her grip on her staff. It tumbled out of the sky in one direction as Gwyllion spun in the other.

"Noooooo! Boris! Help me!" she screamed. A moment later, she hit the ground—hard. She moaned as her staff landed next to her, breaking into two pieces.

At the very moment the staff broke,

Mariposa felt Gwyllion's magic release its hold on her. She could move again! She scrambled to her feet and raced toward Catania. "You made it!" she cried happily.

"Not fast enough," Catania countered. "It's too late. Look." She pointed toward the Heartstone.

A hideous black stain of evil magic seeped across the front of the stone, pulsing bigger and bigger. Mariposa shuddered. It wouldn't be long before the Heartstone was extinguished completely.

Catania was near tears. "It's so cold," the princess said, her voice trembling as the Heartstone began to shudder and shake.

Mariposa looked toward the horizon, where the sun had slipped behind a last cloud. She shivered. It was so dark and so cold without the warmth and glow of the Heartstone. What would the Crystal Fairies do now?

Just then, Mariposa noticed something glowing beneath the fabric of Catania's skirt. "Catania, look!" she cried.

Catania glanced down and gasped. "Oh! The Flutter Flower!" She pulled the flower out of her pocket and held it up. Then she saw her Crystallite necklace start to glow.

Mariposa cocked her head in thought. "I wonder . . . ," she started. She told Catania to hold the flower close to the Heartstone. The girls waited a minute, feeling hopeful. But nothing happened. "I thought maybe . . ." Mariposa's voice trailed away in disappointment.

Then she noticed a flicker inside the Heartstone. "Wait! Keep holding it close to the Heartstone!" she cried, putting her hand on top of Catania's. Together, they held the flower toward the stone. "It's working!"

Zee and Anu were now unfrozen, too. They jumped up and down excitedly.

The girls smiled, and the glow of the Heartstone grew and grew. The Crystallite pulsed with energy until it almost exploded with a surge of bright, colorful light.

Mariposa shielded her eyes as the burst of energy seemed to light up all of Shimmervale.

The sheer force of the energy pushed Mariposa and Catania back. Dazzled by the spectacle, the two friends watched as every color in the rainbow darted under and around them. The colors even began to change their wings! Both fairies' wings became larger and more colorful, glistening with twinkling, blinking crystals.

"Your wings!" Mariposa exclaimed.

"Your wings!" Catania replied, grinning.

In a flash, the colorful explosion disappeared, leaving the Heartstone glowing just as it had before Gwyllion arrived.

The girls looked out over Shimmervale and smiled as Crystallites all over the city flickered back to life.

Zee and Anu rushed up and admired the girls' new wings. *Ooh! Ahh!*

Catania reached into her pocket and handed the friendship necklace back to Mariposa. Mariposa was thrilled to have it back. Things were looking brighter already!

Chapter 17

Mariposa, Catania, Sylvie, Zee, and Anu flew down from the palace rooftops together. Catania looked around for the king, who came racing out of the palace to greet her.

"Father!" she cried, gliding toward him.

"Catania! You're flying!" exclaimed the king.

The two hugged each other, and then the king held Catania at arm's length.

"Your wings. . . . They're beautiful!"

Catania twirled. "Thank you."

"I'm so, so proud of you. And you, Mariposa," the king said. "I owe you an apology. I misjudged you. I was wrong."

Mariposa smiled warmly. But before she could answer, they heard a voice nearby.

"Mistress, c'mon, get up, eh?" pleaded Boris.

"We still got a chance, you can do this!"

The group rounded the corner to find Gwyllion still lying on the ground.

She stirred, coming to. "Where's my staff?"

The king balled his fists, struggling to contain his rage. "It's gone, Gwyllion. Just like you'll be when I'm done with you. Any last words?"

Catania put her hand on her father's arm. "Father, no. You mustn't harm her."

"What?" the king responded.

"Remember why all this happened," Catania him. "Gwyllion asked us for one Crystallite. One. And we have so many, but we said no."

"And that gives her the right to destroy us?" the king asked, growing angry.

"No, not at all. But destroying her isn't right, either," Catania reasoned.

The king sighed, resigned. "What do you suggest we do?"

"What we should have done in the first place," Catania replied. She knelt down next to Gwyllion. She took off her own Crystallite necklace and held it out to the old woman.

Zee looked questioningly at Mariposa. *What is she doing?*

"She's being a friend," Mariposa replied softly. "And maybe making one, too."

Catania spoke to Gwyllion. "I'm giving you your freedom, and a chance to start over. I know that's not always easy . . . so maybe this will help." She fastened the necklace around the old woman's neck.

Gwyllion looked shocked. "You . . . you're giving me a gift? After everything I did?"

Catania nodded. "I'm righting a wrong."

"I . . . I don't know what to say," Gwyllion stammered. She held the Crystallite charm in her hand, and as she did, a swirl of rainbow magic seeped out and wafted over her. She stood, mystified, as the lines on her face smoothed, her white hair turned brunette, and she became younger and healthier. "Thank you," she said, choked up with emotion. "I hope I can live up to your faith in me."

Gwyllion put an arm around Boris. "Come, my pet. We have much to think about." She bowed to the king and princess and took off into the sky, Boris flapping behind her.

The king turned to Catania. "You may be a child," he said solemnly, "but in some ways you're wiser than I'll ever be."

Catania blushed and hugged him. "Thank you, Father."

Mariposa heard a sudden sniffling and turned to find Zee and Anu hugging and crying into each other's shoulders. She laughed. It looked like everyone was feeling a little choked up by the day's events!

The king faced Mariposa. "I'd like to repay your kindness," he declared.

"Thank you, Your Majesty," she said. Good deeds didn't need to be repaid, Mariposa knew. But she did have an idea. "Hmm, there is one thing you can do for me," she told him with a twinkle in her eye.

Chapter 18

A few days later, back in Flutterfield, Anu and Zee entered the ballroom with their arms linked. Zee grabbed a flower from a nearby table and put it between her teeth. As the music swelled, they began to tango.

Across the ballroom, Carlos introduced King Regellius to his mother. "Mother, this is King Regellius of Shimmervale. King Regellius, my mother, Queen Marabella of Flutterfield."

The king bowed deeply. "Your Majesty," he said. Then, remembering what Mariposa had told him about greetings in Flutterfield, he said, "I mean, 'Hey!'"

Queen Marabella arched an eyebrow, confused. "Hey?"

Satisfied, Carlos flew off.

"May I have this dance?" the king asked.

"You're not concerned about my fire breath?" Queen Marabella asked playfully.

King Regellius blushed. "Your Majesty, I am ashamed that I ever thought—"

The queen waved off his apology. "Our myths about you were just as silly. But it's all in the past now. It's a privilege to have you here!"

"And I wanted to give you this," the king said, reaching into his robe pocket. "An offering of peace and goodwill." He handed the queen a shimmering necklace.

"Is that a Crystallite?" the queen asked, marveling at the necklace. "It's even more beautiful than Mariposa described. Thank you."

"You're welcome," the king replied. "Now, may I have this dance?"

"Why, yes," the queen answered, holding out her hand. "I'd love to."

The king led her onto the dance floor, passing Mariposa, Catania, Carlos, Willa, and Talayla.

"No way!" Willa said, slapping her knee.

"Watch!" Mariposa exclaimed. She folded

her wings down and eyed Catania. "Ready?"

"Ready," Catania replied, folding her wings down, skirt-style.

On the count of three, the girls curtsied and their wings flew up. *Sproing!*

Everyone broke out laughing, even Sylvie, who sat quietly noshing on a bale of hay behind them. Her wing was wrapped carefully in a rainbow-colored bandage.

"Seriously?" Willa asked. "You knocked the king's crown off his head with your wing? Whoa!"

"Well, it was an accident!" Mariposa insisted, giggling. It was funny, looking back on it now.

"I'd never seen his face that red," Catania confirmed.

"I have," Talayla inserted. "But not since I accidentally put lava sauce in his fluffle muffins. I'll never live *that* down!"

"Ew!" Mariposa, Catania, and Willa shouted at the same time.

With all the catching up they'd been doing, Mariposa had almost forgotten the most important question of all. She turned to Willa and Carlos. "How'd everything go at the library? Still standing, I hope?"

Carlos and Willa exchanged a look.

"Are you kidding?" Willa said cheerfully. "It was a breeze. Easy as flutterbutter!"

Just then, a Butterfly Fairy breezed by and recognized Willa. "Hey! There's that awful tour guide!" she said to her friend.

"Yeah, we want our money back!" the friend agreed.

Willa blushed. "Uh-oh. I . . . uh . . . have to . . . uh . . . freshen up," she stammered, making a beeline for the bathroom.

Mariposa raised an eyebrow. But Carlos only winked and gave her a thumbs-up. Then he put his arm around her shoulder and said, "I just wanted to tell you again how impressed I am by everything you accomplished."

Catania and Talayla exchanged a look, smiling mischievously. They took off toward the snack table, leaving Carlos and Mariposa alone.

"Thank you, Carlos," Mariposa replied. "I

couldn't have done it without the Flutter Flower."

"Care to dance?" Carlos asked nervously.

Mariposa grinned. "I'd love to."

"See? What did I tell you?" Catania whispered to Talayla at the snack table. "Made for each other!"

Willa joined them from the bathroom, having escaped her angry tourists. "What'd I miss?" she asked the girls.

Then they heard someone clearing his throat nearby. They turned to see Lord Gastrous approaching.

"Well," he said to Catania and Talayla, "I can see clearly that my ideas of Crystal Fairies were far-fetched indeed! You are in no way vicious or vile."

Catania struggled to hide her smile "Why, thank you, Lord Gastrous."

Willa and Talayla tried to keep from laughing.

The band swung into high gear, playing a super-upbeat tune.

"Ohh! I love this song!" Willa exclaimed. She turned to Catania. "Do you dance?"

Catania grinned. "Yes!" she replied.

"Then come on!" Willa cried, and led Catania and Talayla into the dance area.

The girls started dancing next to Carlos and Mariposa, and then Willa zipped back to the snack table. She tugged on Lord Gastrous's arm. "You want to get your groove on to this song, Lord Gastrous?" she asked.

Lord Gastrous looked flustered. "What? No! I . . . uh . . . never . . ."

But it was no use—Willa dragged him to the dance floor.

After all, it was never too late to try something new.

As Mariposa twirled and laughed with Catania at the dance, she thought about the past week and all she had learned. She had been so used to getting her answers from books that she'd never realized maybe the most important answers came from the heart instead. New friendships and new adventures were right at her fingertips—all it took was a little courage.

Mariposa clutched her own Crystallite necklace and smiled, then continued dancing with her new friend.

Sparkle

Barbie

Let your dreams

Always be

Let the

Fly &

Sparkle,

A pri

eat fairy princess in you!

adventure lead the way!

Believe in yourself

Shimmer, Flutter!

A Princess Never Hides Her Wings

If you b

To M

If you believe it, you will Soar!

Be A Friend,

Love the Sparkle

To Make A Friend,

Barbie

Wings

Let yo

Sparkle,

The secret to a great friendship

is being a great friend!

Bel

The adventure

Wings

dreams soar!

ys be true to the real fairy princess

Believe